Reluctant Runaway

E. J. Davis

Lutheran Publishing House

Dedicated to
Jim, Kerry, and Leigh,
with love.

Cover and story illustrations: Ron Lisle
First printing August 1989
Second printing January 1990

National Library of Australia
Cataloguing-in-Publication entry

Davis, E.J. (Elizabeth Jane), 1951–
Reluctant runaway.

ISBN 0 85910 475 3.

I. Title.

A823′.3

Printed and published by
Lutheran Publishing House,
205 Halifax Street, Adelaide, South Australia. LPH 1483-89

CHAPTER 1

They had landed on the school oval, three of them, long, sleek, and torpedo-shaped. They stood in a precise triangle, glowing softly in the afternoon sun. All about the school, people stood, watching, silent, terrified. Yet the call for someone — anyone — to go forward and meet the aliens, was still unanswered. Then, suddenly, a small boy walked out of the school building. He was chewing some gum in a couldn't-care-less sort of way, and looked no more concerned about approaching the alien spacecraft than he would have about approaching the school buses. Everyone gasped. The art teacher called out to him, but he ignored her. There were odd sounds coming from the spacecraft, and, as he drew nearer, the boy thought he knew what the sound was; but surely, it couldn't be ... laughter? It was.

Corey Green's eyes shot back into focus as he realized that he had been caught daydreaming again. Miss Malone stopped shaking him and stood, hands on hips, lips tight with exasperation. The laughter quietened to a few sniggers and a giggle or two.

'You've done absolutely nothing this entire lesson, Corey Green. It really is high time you buckled down and did some work', she said.

Art did not stir anything creative in Corey at all, and today they were to make tall skinny things like cranes and giraffes and towers. It was plain boring.

'I don't know what to make', he complained, already determined to refuse every suggestion that Miss Malone might make. But she didn't make any.

'You have exactly two minutes to find some materials from the resource room and get cracking on a model, or else you'll be off to the headmaster's office', she threatened.

There was no evading an ultimatum like that, so Corey wearily climbed to his feet and shuffled dejectedly toward the resource room. To his absolute disgust, Miss Malone followed him.

'Right, Corey, what materials are you going to use? Quickly now, you haven't got all day', she said.

Corey looked around at the uninspiring array of boxes, cardboard, string, glue, coloured paper, and other artistic building equipment. His mind was working fast. What could he make that was tall and skinny, that wouldn't take much time to do, and that would at least keep Miss Malone from breathing down his neck for the rest of the lesson?

'Some string and that box . . .' he muttered, pointing. An old Indian rope trick — that would be tall and skinny. If he could only work out how to hold the rope up, it would solve everything. He wished he knew how it was done.

Miss Malone passed the string and a cardboard box to the boy, and followed him out of the resource room. Corey couldn't think of a way to hold the rope up in the air without building a tower to hang it from, and that was exactly what he was trying to avoid. Pity he wasn't a snake charmer, he thought, peering into the box.

It wasn't empty. Something was rattling around inside the box. At first Corey had ignored it, thinking that it was more useless artistic stuff, but now he saw that it was a tiny cap gun. It was so small that it could easily be hidden in his closed hand, yet he knew that this sort of cap gun was capable of making some very loud noises. He'd seen them before. There was a plastic square in the box too, with rows of little plastic cups held to it by little plastic spot-welds. The caps. There was nearly half a row left.

Smiling secretly to himself, Corey made his way to an unoccupied desk and for ten minutes worked very industriously at cutting long strips of cardboard from one side of the box. Miss Malone watched him suspiciously for a while, but before long her attention was claimed elsewhere, and Corey sat down. He stood the remains of the box on the desk in front of him for cover, and then brought out the tiny cap gun. He broke one of the little plastic cups from its plastic spot-weld, and fixed it in place behind the hammer. Should he fire it?

Julie Parson's dark head bobbed about at desk level in front of him where she was working on her project. On impulse, Corey's arm crept along his desk, alongside the cardboard box toward the dark head. The tiny gun pointed just over the girl's shoulder as she leant back, and then, suddenly, a loud crack split the air.

'What was that?' someone asked.

Julie stood up, her eyes round and big as saucers. For a moment she just stood there, stock-still, half bent as if she might be going to be sick. Then gradually her hands began to move in a flapping motion; they flapped harder and harder, and then she began to scream.

'I can't hear, I can't hear anything.'

Corey was horrified. So was everyone else. Miss Malone went to Julie and tried hard to calm her down, but nothing, it seemed, would work. The girl screamed and screamed and screamed, until Miss Malone finally had to slap her face. Julie just cried then.

'What's going on here!' demanded Mr Perrin, the teacher from next door.

Apart from Julie's crying, there was suddenly a silence so complete that Corey was sure he could hear his own heart beating.

'I think Corey Green is at the bottom of this', Miss Malone said with a sharp look in his direction. 'Can you hear anything now, Julie?'

Sobbing, Julie nodded her head.

'It was a mistake, sir . . . I didn't mean it to go off.'

'Good grief, lad, did you fire that thing in someone's ear?'

Corey looked down and said nothing.

'Don't you know any better by now? What if you've done irreparable damage? What if she's deaf from now on, and all because of you and your cap gun?'

Corey still had nothing to say. He stole a glance at Julie, who was still crying. Miss Malone looked white. He looked back at Mr Perrin, who pointed silently to the doorway. Corey turned and went out, with Mr Perrin following very close behind him.

The headmaster was furious. He gave Corey a very loud and thorough piece of his mind, and finished up by telling him to do 500 lines and hand them in tomorrow morning, first thing. There was also a threat: 'If I have the misfortune of seeing you again this week, for any kind of misbehaviour, then be prepared for a caning, young Green, because I'm sick and tired of you and your trouble-making. It's time you exercised some self-discipline and grew up a bit.'

With that, the headmaster sent him back to class. Art had finished, and Religious Instruction (or RI, as everyone called it) had begun.

The RI teacher was new. His name was Mr Williams, and he was huge — but not fat or old, as most RI teachers were. He was even taller than Mr Perrin, and had a bushy black beard and sharp blue eyes that pierced like twin lasers. His voice was deep, and his hands were the biggest hands Corey had ever seen on any man.

Mr Williams began the lesson by explaining about the New Testament — how it was an account of Jesus' life before he died, and what happened afterwards — and Corey immediately lost interest. Mr Williams might be impressive to look at, but he went on and on about exactly the same things Corey's old RI teacher had gone on about — *and* the minister, *and* his parents for that matter — and to Corey it was all a load of rubbish.

Mr Williams was not a person to put up with nonsense, however, and twice he sternly warned the lad to get on with the work set for him. When, nearly at the end of the lesson, Corey had only one line of writing done, Mr Williams told him to take his book and go and explain it to the headmaster.

A shock wave of fear surged through Corey, and he turned very pale. He hadn't expected this at all. Dumb with shock, unable to move, he swallowed hard and sat staring at Mr Williams. There was no anger in the teacher's face; in fact, he looked quite sorry, but at the same time he still expected Corey to go.

With trembling legs, Corey stood up and walked blindly to the door and out of the classroom. When he got outside, a large tear welled up in each eye and rolled down his cheeks. Quickly he dashed the tears away, but others came to take their place. He hadn't meant to be lazy. It was just that RI was so boring. He couldn't understand how it was going to do him any good when he grew up anyway, and he hadn't been cheeky or rude or anything like that. Feeling numb, he walked across the courtyard to the headmaster's office, but when he reached the door he stopped, unable to bring himself to knock.

'What if you just wait here and don't go in?' a tiny voice in his head said. 'Mr Williams hasn't come with you. He'll never know . . .'

Corey glanced back to the classroom he had just left. There by the window was Mr Williams, watching. Corey turned and knocked, steeling himself to face the headmaster for the second time that day.

He had never had the cane before, and afterwards he felt that he had never hurt so much in all his life. He didn't even bother to wipe the tears from his eyes as he came back into the classroom, and everyone turned to stare as he entered. Corey hung his head so that they wouldn't see.

'Come over here', said Mr Williams. 'The rest of you can go. It's early, but we'll call it an early minute.'

Quickly the children packed away their books and pencils, put their chairs up, and flew out of the classroom with whoops of joy loud enough to let the rest of the school know that

Year Six was out early.

Mr Williams sat down on a desk and pointed Corey into a chair. Corey sat.

'Well, how was it?' Mr Williams asked gently.

'How was what?' Corey returned sullenly.

'Your second trip to the headmaster. I didn't know that you'd already been once today. Your face gave something away, and after one or two questions to your classmates I heard about the cap gun.'

Corey looked up for the first time since coming back into the classroom. Mr Williams's piercing blue eyes were, amazingly, quite gentle.

'I got the cuts', he said simply.

'I'm sorry. But even if I'd known about the previous visit to the headmaster I would have still sent you again', he said.

Corey was silent. He looked down again. Mr Williams wasn't playing fair. If he'd yelled and ranted it would have been OK, but right now he was just making Corey feel as if he wanted to cry.

'Tell me, what makes a good working dog good?' Mr Williams asked.

'Training?' Corey answered.

'Exactly. What good is a dog if it doesn't know what to do when it's needed? If you can't rely on it, it's useless. They have to have discipline or they do what they like, and that's not always good for them, is it? People aren't much different really.'

Still Corey said nothing.

‘Well, you’ve had a bad day by all accounts’, sighed Mr Williams. ‘When you get home, try asking the Lord to show you why today was like it was. Maybe he’ll explain it to you. OK Corey, you can go now.’

Corey stood up, but he was feeling very heavy inside. Quietly he collected his books and bag, put his chair up on his desk, and made his way slowly outside to the area where all the children lined up to catch their buses. He didn’t feel much like talking or messing around, and was glad when he was finally on the bus and going home.

The journey seemed to take for ever, and the heavy feeling did not leave Corey as he neared the farm where he lived. Dejectedly, he climbed off the bus at his stop, and, dragging his knapsack along in the dirt behind him, made his way up the drive. His two brothers and his sister tore ahead, eager to reach home, change, and go out to play. The boys would start kicking goals between the two gum trees in the paddock behind the house, and Linda would be shooting goals through the ancient rusty goal-ring which was fixed somehow to a dead pine tree in the back yard.

For once Corey didn’t feel like playing. He’d never been so upset by trouble before, and he wondered why it was bothering him so much now. He pushed his way dejectedly into the house, and went straight to his room. Maybe if he pretended that he was sick Mum would keep him home tomorrow. He flopped down on to his bed and stared at the wall.

'Corey? Corey, where are you?' It was his mother.

'Here', he said flatly.

'Well, come here. I want a word with you', she said, and by the tone of her voice Corey knew that it meant more trouble. He sighed, got up, and made his way to the kitchen.

Trouble it was. His mother stood by the sink with a letter in her hand, and a stern, annoyed look on her face. She handed the letter to Corey, and he read it through quickly. It was from the headmaster, briefly explaining all Corey's misdemeanours that day, and asking if Mr and Mrs Green would mind dropping by the school one day the following week to discuss the matter. Linda or one of the others must have been given the letter to bring home.

They hadn't said a word, the rotten traitors.

Corey looked up at his mother. She was indeed very cross with him. 'Go to your room, Corey. We'll talk about this when your father comes home', she said.

Tears again sprang to Corey's eyes as he turned and went to his room. She didn't even want to hear his side. This was the worst day he'd ever lived through. Nobody cared about him, they all picked on him, they all wanted to punish him. It wasn't enough that he'd already had the cuts and still had 500 lines to do, they *all* had to have a go. And what would Dad say? He lay on his bed and cried till there were no more tears left. Then, feeling horribly numb inside, he made a decision. He would run away. He'd go to Melbourne or Sydney or ... — well, anywhere away from here. He'd make a fortune and show them all. He'd make them all feel horrible for treating him this way, and what was more, he'd go now, before his father came home.

With this solemn resolve he set about taking all his school books out of his knapsack and putting in it all the things he thought he'd need. An extra jumper, some jeans, a pocket-knife, a torch. He couldn't get to the kitchen for food, but he had some money in his savings tin, so he threw that in too. After a last quick look round his room, he opened the window and climbed out on to the verandah. There was no sign of anyone. Mum was still inside. The others would be playing footy, and Linda was nowhere to be seen. Half ducking, he ran around the side of the house to the front, and, keeping to the oleander bushes which lined the drive, he made his way down to the main road, where he turned and set off with grim determination and a heavy heart on his way south-east. And he hadn't even left a note.

CHAPTER 2

It was just over two kilometres from the farm where Corey lived to the next town, which lay on the West Coast of South Australia some 600 kilometres from Adelaide. Because the town was so close to the Greens' farm, no one thought it odd to see young Corey making his way along the road, knapsack on his back, toward the town.

Several neighbours waved as they passed going in the opposite direction, and when the old Holden pulled up beside him, Corey wasn't particularly worried that anyone would guess he was running away. He didn't recognize the car, and nor could he see the driver, until he came up level with the passenger-side window. It was Mr Williams.

'Going to town?' the big man queried.

'Yeah', answered Corey. He didn't really want to talk to Mr Williams, but he couldn't do anything else without seeming a bit strange.

'Hop in. I'll drive you there', he offered.

Silently Corey opened the door, slipped his knapsack on to the seat, and climbed in after it, slamming the door shut behind him. The old Holden roared, and Mr Williams leant out of his window to see along the road behind him before pulling out again. There was silence for a few moments, then Mr Williams asked: 'Where do you have to go? That knapsack looks heavy. You're not leaving town, are you?'

Of course, he was only joking, but for one moment Corey froze, his mind working rapidly.

'The drycleaner's', he said finally, patting his knapsack. Mr Williams nodded, and Corey gave a mental sigh of relief.

Within minutes, the car pulled up in front of the drycleaner's, and Corey gathered his knapsack together and opened the door.

'You know', Mr Williams said reflectively, 'when I was your age I remember having a specially bad day, probably a lot like the one you had today.'

'What did you do?' Corey asked, in spite of himself.

'I ran away', said Mr Williams simply.

Corey remained silent.

'Well, at least you're not doing that', the man laughed. 'I thought I could prove everything that way, but the only things it *did* prove were not the ones *I* wanted to prove. Anyway, I must be off. See you next week, OK?'

Corey climbed out thoughtfully, closed the door, and watched as the green Holden drove away. Had Mr Williams guessed that he intended to run away? Perhaps his face was all red and blotchy from crying, or maybe Mr Williams had seen him stiffen when he'd joked about Corey leaving town. Should he go back? Even as the thought crossed his mind, he rejected it. He was in enough trouble at home already, without going back now and adding this to his list.

Purposefully he lifted his pack on to his shoulders, and walked along the street to the local store. Here he bought some biscuits, fritz, and some apples, and put them on the family account. At the newsagent's he bought a litre of Coke, and then he was set. Sighing resolutely, he started off down the street. He had a long way to go, and the sooner he started off the better he would feel about it. An odd reluctance was hanging on him like a heavy weight, and he didn't like it at all.

Trudging slowly, he thought again about the whole day. Starting right from the beginning, when he had got up, he mentally relived everything that had happened to him. He had an uncomfortable feeling that everything had backfired somehow, and blown up into something far bigger than he'd ever expected it to, but it was too late now to turn back.

The day had been hot, even though it was now autumn, and Corey, in only shorts and T-shirt, suddenly felt conscious of the coolness that usually came with evenings at this time of year. His thoughts had occupied him for fully two hours, and he was now well clear of the town. Later he would need his jumper.

His father was probably home now, and Corey wondered whether anyone would look for him tonight, or whether they'd wait until morning. His family would all be sitting around the table, probably having tea. The kitchen windows would be open to catch the breeze, for the house got hot with the sort of weather they'd had this week. Dad would read the paper, and then Mum would tell him about today; probably she would be a bit worried. Then they'd have tea, all of them, very quietly, while Dad 'nutted' his way through the problem, as he'd say, and then after some prayers and his second cup of tea he'd announce his decision on what was to be done.

Corey could picture the whole thing in his mind. Just as when the neighbours had come and told them they'd caught Dad's best sheep-dog mauling their sheep. And when young Paul had been caught smoking, and when Linda had let all the sheep out at shearing time because she'd been in too big a hurry to fasten the yard gate properly. Dad was very stern, but Corey had to admit that he always figured things out first and was usually fair. But he was pretty frightening too, when he was really mad. Corey walked faster.

Presently a lone car appeared distantly on the highway, headlights showing palely in the twilight. Corey watched it for a moment, and then suddenly thought of something. If he didn't want to be caught he'd better get off the roadway. Headlights would pick him up here as easily as a spotlight found a rabbit or a roo, and then he wouldn't get very far at all.

He looked around him. The road ran straight ahead, dipping slightly before beginning a long climb to the top of a distant rise. To his right was scrub and some open farmland, to the left a ribbon of wattle and scrub some 30 metres wide, then the dirt track which serviced the Todd water pipeline. Corey turned through the barrier of wattle bushes and gum trees, over rocks and mounds and miniature banks, to the dirt track. Away from the road, with a ribbon of scrub on one side and the huge water pipe and more scrub on the other, Corey knew he would be reasonably safe, but now he felt suddenly cut off. Night was closing in fast, and his ever-lively imagination was already playing tricks on him. Did that stick move, or did it just look that way? It could be a snake; the weather had been warm enough today.

Why was it that bushes moved when there was no breeze, and what was that shape there, way up the track; it would be darker still by the time he reached it.

'Nonsense', he told himself firmly. 'It's just a bush. It's exactly the same at night as it is during the day. Anyway, there aren't any dangerous animals out here except snakes, and they don't come out at night if it's cold.'

He'd felt cool earlier, but now he'd worked himself up into a sweat, partly because he had unconsciously doubled his speed until he was almost running, and partly because he was, just a little, frightened. Despite his firm words to himself, however, his imagination still continued to supply him with more and more horrendous possibilities. Did that star move? He was sure it had changed position from where it had been before. What colour were UFOs? Even if they never wanted to conquer Earth, they probably still needed a few specimens. It was quite dark now, and a boy on his own on a dark lonely track couldn't belong to anyone as far as 'they' were concerned, a great opportunity . . .

What was that bright light up the track to the right a bit, in the scrub? That, certainly, was not his imagination. Like a huge spotlight it shone skywards, shining around as if it was occasionally being pivoted (maybe from a UFO), and for what seemed like an age it hung there, in the air, sometimes moving and sometimes not. A dull low hum could be heard now. Surely it wasn't skimming low over the scrub, 'looking'?

Corey had stopped in his tracks, his eyes wide with fear, and he shivered. Half-uttered words slipped from his lips, and, still watching the mesmerising light above the scrub, he slid his pack off his back. Bringing it round in front of him he hugged it tightly, and, without quite knowing what he was doing, began to step backwards, until he was stopped by one of the concrete supports which held the Todd water pipe. Crickets chirped, and he could hear spooky rustles and movements in the nearby scrub, and all the while the hum grew louder and

louder. Then, quite suddenly, the light was gone.

'O no', Corey groaned, 'they've turned off the lights to make me move, like Dad does with the roos', and he sank to his knees and backed in under the pipe, pressing in next to the rough but comforting solidness of the concrete support, hugging his pack and making himself as small as he possibly could.

The roar was quite loud now, but still the lights didn't shine, and Corey desperately needed some reassurance. Rocking gently backwards and forwards, he uttered over and over again: 'I don't want to go, I don't want to go, don't let them take me God, O please, don't let them take me.'

Staring wide-eyed ahead of him toward the main road, which he had quite forgotten was so close, he could hear the roar of a powerful engine as it came closer. Then suddenly, through the trees the lights reappeared. Illuminating the highway, a huge semi-trailer screamed past in a flash of bright spotlights, headlights, sidelights, and tail-lights, and Corey sank like a pricked balloon as recognition and realization crept into his terrified brain. It had been the semi's lights shining upward as it climbed the long hill from the other side that Corey had seen. He couldn't even cry; neither could he bring himself to leave his little hideaway.

Shivering with reaction and cold, he opened

his pack and pulled out his jumper and jeans. It took a long time to put them on where he sat, but he couldn't make himself climb out for anything. Wishing he'd brought a blanket, he settled down to one of the coldest, loneliest, and longest nights he'd ever known.

CHAPTER 3

Very early the next morning, in a grey half-light, Corey woke to the sound of something thumping. He opened his eyes, and cautiously peered out through a fine mist on to the track. Not four metres away was the biggest buck kangaroo he had ever seen. It had stopped its journey along the track and now sat up, sniffing the air as if it sensed another presence. The animal was huge, far taller than Corey's father, who was nearly two metres, and although it didn't appear alarmed it was certainly alert, its sensitive ears twitching. Its forepaws were half lifted and held as if they'd been about to scratch, but were waiting until the ears were satisfied about the safety of the track before continuing with their job.

Although Corey wasn't afraid of kangaroos, and knew that usually they would flee rather than fight, he had learnt some valuable lessons from his father. A buck kangaroo at certain times of the year could be as unpredictable and dangerous as one of Africa's water buffalo. 'Always wait it out, Corey. If there's a doe around, then don't tangle with them. They could rip you apart in minutes.'

Corey sat very still, and sure enough, a moment later, a smaller roo bounded out of the scrub and up to the buck. The boy held his breath and watched, chewing his lip a little with apprehension, but the kangaroos turned together, as if by some instinct or secret sign, and suddenly bounded off down the track, through the scrub and away.

Stiffly, Corey climbed out from under the Todd pipe and wriggled his cramped feet and legs. He felt worn out, numb with cold and very hungry, but at least with the daylight he wasn't frightened any more.

The long, cold, lonely night, however, had done its work well, and Corey was having some very serious second thoughts now about running away.

He didn't even want to think about another night like the one he'd just been through, yet it was obvious that he would have to put together some sort of plan. He had no idea how far he was from his home town, and nor did he know what time of day it was, but even now his pride was telling him that he wasn't quite far enough away to make an impression. He didn't ever want to let on that he had been afraid of the dark, and that that was why he came home. No, he would have to be 'found'. Mildinna was the next township on, and Corey had an aunt there. If he was to be 'accidentally' spotted by her when she went to meet her own children from their school bus that afternoon, then that would solve everything. It shouldn't take too long to cover the distance to Mildinna, and yet it was far enough away to let people know he really had meant business.

Feeling extremely satisfied with this plan of action, Corey had a quick breakfast of fritz and stale biscuits, hoisted his pack on to his back, and set off once more. The air was sharp and chill, and he found that his nose was stinging with a tingle that made his eyes water. It wasn't quite frosty, but it was horribly cold.

Yet even as he travelled, Corey was plagued by conflicting thoughts. It was all very well to allow himself to be found, but what was he going back to? He hadn't done his 500 lines, his parents would still be wild about the letter from the headmaster, Julie might still not be able to hear properly, and now there was running away to add to the list. On the other hand, he couldn't face another night like the one he'd had last night.

Early as it was, the sun shone brightly, promising another warm day. In the distance, the drone of a car coming along the highway alerted him to the possibilities of being caught too soon. He wasn't ready for that yet. He looked around, and the huge Todd water pipe on his left gave him an idea. Resting on its concrete supports, it was, where the ground dipped, half a metre or so off the ground, quite high enough for Corey to climb under. On the other side he could count on being shielded by both the pipe and the scrub that grew on the other side of it.

He scrambled under the pipe, and on the other side he set off quickly. The sooner he reached the next town the better, he thought.

It was nearly an hour later when Corey came upon a rest area. It was just a gravelled patch, with an access track from the highway at both ends and a large concrete rubbish-bin in the centre. A huge semi-trailer stood silently under the gum trees, waiting.

Nothing moved. Corey climbed under the Todd pipe again and quietly moved closer, eyeing the huge rig. It was a terrific semi, and he was very impressed. As he came closer, it suddenly struck him that if he had really intended to go to Sydney or Melbourne and not just to Mildinna, then this would be the way to do it, on the back of a semi.

He couldn't resist the impulse to go up close and have a better look. Carefully looking around, he strained his ears for a full minute before stepping out into the open.

The tray was very high up; in fact, the wheels were quite as high as Corey himself, and there were no steps anywhere that he could see, except a kind of steel ladder attached to the side of the cabin. No one jumped up or spoke; everything was quiet. Perhaps the driver was asleep in the cabin. Corey certainly hoped so. As quietly as possible, he made his way along the side of the semi. His heart was hammering inside his chest, and he found that his hands were trembling as he adjusted his pack on his back. The semi's cargo was some sort of machinery, the likes of which Corey had never seen before, and it was held secure with chains and ropes and huge wedges of wood, which sat behind each wheel.

Corey looked around again, half expecting to see the driver watching him openly from some wide open space, just as in the movies, but no one was there. The first rung of the ladder was so high up that Corey had to climb on to the step to the cabin door first, and then reach over to the ladder. The steel rung was icy cold and slightly damp, and Corey shivered as much from excitement as from cold. What would he do if the driver woke up? But he'd never really had a close look at a semi before.

It was now, while Corey was working out how, if he should ever want to run away again in the future, he could get from the cabin steps to the trailer itself, that two things happened, sending shock waves up and down his spine.

First there was a rattle, a loud burst of static from inside the cabin of the rig, and a man's voice suddenly answering it; and then there was the arrival of a police car.

Undecided, Corey hung on to the rung of the ladder with one foot on the step to the cabin and the other wavering in the air as he considered his next move. It was plain that he couldn't stay there; the driver might find him at any moment. On the other hand, if he jumped down and ran for cover, the police in the car, which was even now pulling up on the other side of the rig, might see him and catch him. It had never occurred to him that the police would be involved in this. Could this mean that he would have a record if he was caught? Mum and Dad must be really wild.

Corey could hear the men talking as plainly as if he had been in the cab with them.

'G'day.'

'G'day.'

'We're on the lookout for a runaway kid. Eleven or twelve years, average height, stocky build, blond hair, blue eyes, carrying a blue school pack. Name's Corey Green. Haven't seen anyone like that between towns, have you?'

'Nope, can't say's I have.'

'Doubt if he's got this far really, unless he's got a lift. Probably turn up at some relatives later on in the day. Anyhow, if you spot him . . .'

'Yeah sure, I'll buzz you on the two-way.'

'Thanks.'

'No worries, see you', and suddenly a loud roar split the morning silence, a long shudder vibrated through the vehicle, and in sheer surprise Corey nearly lost what precious hold he had. Obviously the driver was ready to begin his journey. The enormous diesel engine throbbed as it warmed up, and Corey realized that if he didn't scramble up the ladder now he would be left standing alone, facing the police car.

With the hissing of compressed air and the gentle thunder of the engine tearing at the morning's quiet, Corey made up his mind, and just as the rig was put into gear he swung and pulled himself up on to the ladder proper. The rig moved off. Hanging on tightly, Corey reached his foot over on to the tray, followed it with his other foot, and landed safely by the huge wheel of the machine on the back. Quickly he dropped into a sitting position behind the wheel, so that any view of him from the police car would be obscured. Corey watched with a mixed sense of relief and hopelessness as the police car pulled out from the rest area, turned, and headed back toward home. He'd escaped the police, but where on earth was he going now?

CHAPTER 4

Stealing away on a semi-trailer would have been the perfect answer to all of Corey's immediate problems, had he really intended to continue running away, but in reality the adventure wasn't at all exciting. For one thing, he couldn't see where he was going, and though he desperately wanted to peer through the window at the back of the cab, he couldn't bring himself to do it for fear that the driver might catch sight of him in the rear-vision mirror.

The rig moved with incredible speed for such a large vehicle, and the machinery on the back groaned and strained, creaked and moaned, as it fidgeted fretfully against its bonds. At first Corey wondered if it was safe, and for a long time watched very closely for any sign that the ropes and chains were loosening their hold somewhere, but gradually his confidence grew and he realized that nothing dreadful was going to happen after all.

The groans, moans, and creaks had in fact fallen into a kind of rhythm, which was only disturbed on odd occasions when another vehicle flashed past in the other direction. The sun shone brightly now from a blue cloudless sky, and though there had been very little breeze that morning Corey now found it definitely draughty. Little gusts of wind darted and puffed at him from around the machinery, and two steady draughts curled almost visibly around either side of the cab to come rushing together at exactly the place where he sat. But worse than anything else was the fact that he was being carried, absolutely against all his wishes, further away from his home than he had ever been before, and Corey was desperately worried.

The rig travelled on and on and on, and though it was cold and uncomfortable, the rhythmic movements finally succeeded in lulling Corey into a kind of half sleep. But it wasn't a very satisfying sleep.

When he roused himself again, he saw by the sun that it was well past midday. He shifted his position stiffly, and wondered vaguely what it was that had made him wake up so suddenly. And then he knew. They were slowing down.

Now wide awake, Corey crawled to the edge of the tray and peered around the side for a glimpse of what lay ahead. The semi was still travelling at a reasonable speed, and the road ahead was curving to the left through flat farming country. Corey's blond hair whipped back flat against his head and then pointed out behind as the wind caught it, and he had to screw up his eyes and squint to see. As they rounded the bend, a small township came into view and a signpost leapt forward to meet them: Port Wakefield.

Corey sat back again and thought rapidly, as the driver changed a gear and the semi slowed down some more. It was obvious that it was soon going to stop, and Corey intended getting off as quickly as possible. Another gear change, and the rig growled and hissed as its speed was checked. They passed a roadhouse, and the semi braked again, and then began to turn in at the next roadhouse, hardly moving now as it crawled along to a suitable place for parking. Corey looked down, and though the ground seemed a long way off he decided that it was now he must jump, or never. Half standing and half crouching, he waited; then, just as the rig finally came to a halt, he jumped.

The ground was hard as Corey fell and rolled, but he was quickly on his feet again and running. As far as he could tell, nobody had seen him. There were plenty of cars and trucks, even a few other semis, and people were milling here and there between their vehicles and the roadhouses, but no one, it seemed, took any notice of Corey. Hunger rattled in his stomach as he came up to the restaurant section, and the smell of frying onions and coffee hung in the air. He'd not eaten since very early that morning, and now, suddenly, food was the most important and comforting thing he could think of. As he pushed open the door, his stomach growled emptily and his mouth watered. Quickly he dug through his pack and found his savings tin. There were still some biscuits, fritz, and an apple left, but they were as unappetizing as cardboard compared to the smells in here. A plump lady with black curly hair and a pin-prick pair of eyes asked him what he wanted.

'A bucket of chips and a hot dog with loads of sauce', he told her unhesitatingly.

The woman said nothing, but turned back to the kitchen to organize the order. Corey sat down at an empty table and counted the money from his tin. There wasn't much there, about five dollars and some change.

Corey was wondering what he could do next, when the waitress arrived with two steaming parcels, so Corey pushed his problems aside and settled down to eat. When he'd finished, though, his worries about what to do returned. It was after 4 o'clock, and the only solution Corey could think of was to climb aboard another rig heading west, toward home, and just hope that he would be able to get off somewhere near Mildinna, or perhaps even near his own place.

The thought of Perth crossed his mind unbidden, and the horrifying possibility of his being overcarried so far sent shivers playing up and down his spine. But what else could he do?

Ring up?

It was a tempting thought. But what would he say? Tell them he was sorry? He wasn't really. After all, the very reason he'd run away was to teach them all a lesson.

'Why don't you just say that you phoned to

tell them you're OK?' a voice in his head seemed to suggest.

Now, that idea was a good one. Mum was always going on about being considerate to other people.

Corey stood up and went to the counter, and the lady came immediately.

'Is there a phone box here somewhere?' he asked.

'No, love, but there's a public phone in the other roadhouse just before this one.'

'Thanks', Corey said, and turned for the door.

The other roadhouse was bigger, and also very busy. Corey pushed through the glass door into the back of a crowd of people, all jostling and talking and waiting to be served. He looked around, and spotted the phone almost immediately. It was on the wall at the far side of the restaurant, in full view of everyone. Even if the roadhouse had been empty, Corey realized that he could never make the call on that phone. What if some customers came in, and what about the people who worked there? Quickly he turned for the door and left. His only hope, then, was to try and get aboard another semi. Even semis had to stop somewhere for fuel, he reasoned.

So there it was. With the decision made, Corey now had to find himself another lift. However, it was one thing to jump off a semi just as it pulled in, but to climb aboard another one, in broad daylight, in front of a roadhouse, would be an entirely different matter. Rigs were passing through all the time, and quite often two or three together would pull in and park, one behind the other in a long line, rather like a massive train without rails. Many of them were carrying machinery or cars or crates, while others were covered with enormous green canvases, their cargo a mystery to anyone who was curious. But this was not solving the problem. Corey had to find a way to board one without being noticed, and, remembering the difficulty with which he had clambered aboard the first rig, he had grave doubts as to whether he could manage it a second time without being caught.

The sun gradually disappeared, and darkness crept behind like a stalking cat, and still Corey hung around. The roadhouse lights now glowed palely, and as much as he would have liked to sit inside, he didn't want to draw attention to himself in case someone asked questions. So he sat instead on a small area of grass on the roadside just by the boundary to the driveway, and here he watched carefully for a semi with enough room for a boy and the means for him to climb aboard.

The hours passed as Corey continued to sit and wait. It was after midnight before anything happened. Then, feeling cold and dejected, Corey decided to walk along the road toward the other roadhouses to see if there was any chance of finding a lift there. He saw a convoy come in from the west, and thought rather hopelessly to himself that only a few hours ago these same trucks must have driven past his home.

The convoy was slowing down, and presently began to turn in at the roadhouse Corey had just left. He shrugged. They were all going the wrong way anyway. He kept walking, more to keep warm than because he believed that he would find any opportunities further along the road.

Meanwhile, rig after rig began to line up on the asphalt in front of the restaurant Corey had just left, and when there was no parking space left behind, they began another line alongside, until finally all but the last rig had come to a halt. It seemed that there was no place left for this one to park except for the narrow strip of grass between the road and the asphalt parking area, where Corey had recently been sitting. The driver continued through the driveway, and then, using the whole area, turned a huge U-turn, finally pulling up on the grass with only inches to spare, alongside his companions, but facing in the other direction. It would mean another U-turn back on to the road when they got going again, but at this time of night there would not be much traffic to hold up, if any. And anyway the driver was hungry. Turning off the engine, he climbed down, gave a quick whistle to an enormous black dog which dropped silently to the ground beside him, and then headed for the restaurant. The dog followed and organized itself on the mat just outside the doorway to wait.

When Corey returned, it was chewing contentedly on a large bone, and Corey decided that it was the biggest dog he'd ever seen. But it was only a passing observation. Corey had now spotted the only semi-trailer he'd seen all night which was pointing in the right direction, parked only inches from the convoy which had come in earlier. His heart jumped with hope, and quickly he covered the remaining distance to the two lines of semis. They were indeed parked very close together, and he marvelled that anyone could bring such a huge vehicle so close to another without actually hitting it. This was the chance he'd been waiting for, though. Between the semis Corey was hidden from view from both the road and the restaurant, and by using two of the vehicles as leverage, he was able to haul himself up and on to the rig nearest the road, the only one pointing west for home.

It was huge, and had two storeys, with four new cars chained into place on each level. Corey wondered for a moment where he could hide himself. There was, really, only one place. Quickly he made his way to the side of the car nearest, and tried the rear door. It opened, and immediately the interior light flashed on. Corey slammed the door shut again, and then cursed himself for making a noise. For a full minute he stood rigid, half expecting someone to call him down and ask what he thought he was up to, but no one came. Well, if he could get away with it once, he might manage it again, he decided, and taking a deep breath he pulled open the door a second time, dived inside, and pulled it shut behind him as quickly as possible. Moments passed and still nothing happened. Slowly he let out a long sigh of relief.

It wasn't warm in the car, but it was not nearly as cold as it had been outside. Corey's eyes felt as though they were as wide as saucers, yet they were heavy too, and his head ached a little. O how good it would be to be in his own bed now, home with Mum and Dad . . .

For nearly an hour Corey sat and watched from his hideaway in the car for any sign of the semi driver's return. The thought of them in the restaurant, eating, made his stomach groan, and his mouth watered as he remembered the hot dog he had eaten earlier. Quickly he grabbed his pack, fumbled it open, and plunged his hands into it, searching for the last of the fritz he knew was down there. Loose biscuits crumbled and the empty Coke bottle kept getting in the way, but finally his fingers grasped the lump of meat which was wedged in the corner of his pack. It felt sticky and plastic, and when he brought it to his mouth an odd slimy smell almost made him gag. For a second time he thrust his hand into his pack and scrabbled around to find his torch. Turning its light on to his prospective meal, he recoiled with a leap, throwing the fritz down on to the floor of the car. The skin was indeed slimy, but this was not what had caused Corey's violent reaction; from the open end where he had been about to take his first mouthful, there was a writhing honeycomb of tiny maggots, deeply embedded into the fritz. Corey's appetite fled. His lips curled with revulsion as he bent to pick up the fritz, and his toes curled as his fingers closed. With his left hand he wound down the window and furiously tossed the horrible lump of meat from the car, then he turned the torch back on to the floor and began picking up the squirming maggots which had dropped from the fritz. Corey's insides squirmed too. Ugh!

At last, when every maggot he could find was done away with, Corey settled back with a sigh. Presently, voices drifted from the restaurant and gradually grew louder as the group of drivers returned. No one checked his cargo, and as the last semi swung around in another U-turn and set off east, no one had any idea that it carried an extra passenger, curled up in a most uncomfortable position and already sound asleep.

CHAPTER 5

Corey was feeling sick. It seemed hours since he had last eaten, and he found himself alternately both longing for and dreading the first mouthful. He couldn't face the biscuits in his pack, partly because he was sick of biscuits and partly because he remembered the maggots which had been in there.

Yet the semi-trailers still travelled, and Corey wished desperately that they would stop. Already he had realized that his plans had gone terribly wrong. He didn't recognize the country; he had no idea where he was, and he was feeling very frightened.

Another natural need was also making itself known, and with each passing kilometre it was becoming more and more urgent. If the rigs didn't stop soon, he would be in grave danger of having an accident. This serious problem led to more possibilities as Corey considered things. If the semi did in fact stop soon, in broad daylight, then however was he going to get off without being caught? And once he was caught, what would he say? On the other hand, the only alternative was to stay in the car and wet himself. He decided that he'd rather be caught than do that.

Corey sighed, a frown creasing his forehead.

He didn't know which problem was the worst, his urgent need for relief, the wave of nausea which kept returning alternately with pangs of hunger, or the fact that he was a very long way from home.

'O Lord', he groaned aloud, 'they have to stop soon, they have to', and he clasped his knees tightly together, folded his arms across his stomach, and leant forward, trying desperately to stop all the discomforts which were screaming at him through his mind and through his body.

And the semi did stop. Although it seemed an age to Corey, it was little more than five minutes before the great vehicle began to change gears and slow down.

A surge of hope rose in Corey, along with a surge of hunger, and clasping his pack he opened the door of the car an inch or two, ready to jump out as quickly as he could.

With the hissing of air-brakes and the rhythmic thrum of the diesel, the rig turned at last and pulled up in a parking bay behind a long line of others. Uncaring and unable to wait any longer, Corey climbed from the car, dragging his pack behind him, stepped to the edge of the semi, and jumped.

The jump was nearly disastrous, but he managed to hold on until he got around to the other side, where he took off at a run for the nearest bush. A shout rang out, and a dog barked.

‘Hold him, Luke’, someone yelled, and from the passenger window of the very rig Corey had been travelling on, the huge and almost liquid form of a dog leapt to the chase.

But Corey wasn’t afraid of dogs, no matter how big they were, and this one only reminded him of his father’s kangaroo dog at home, except that it was bigger. Anyway, nothing, not even a huge black roo dog, or whatever it was, was going to make Corey embarrass himself. Behind the bush as the dog caught up to him, Corey swung around and, just as he always did to his father’s dog when it got too excited, slapped the creature firmly on the nose and told it to sit down until he was finished.

In sheer surprise, the massive creature did exactly as it was told, and it was still sitting in surprised obedience when the semi driver rounded the bush in pursuit.

Sullenly Corey looked up, and then turned his back, but not before he’d felt a shock of surprise himself. The driver was a giant of a man, and although anger had been on his face to begin with, this had immediately melted into a very quick humour when he saw Corey. The laughter which bubbled so readily into his eyes as he saw Corey’s plight was only slightly dampened when he noticed his dog, sitting obediently beside the boy as if he’d known him all his life. ‘Come, Luke’, the man commanded, and the dog got up and went to him.

Corey turned and stood waiting. There really

wasn't much point in trying to run this time; even if the dog hadn't held him before, there was no saying that it wouldn't do the job properly the next time. And looking at this giant a few metres away, Corey had no doubts at all that this huge man could catch him if he wanted to. He'd never seen anyone quite that big before, except for Mr Williams, but while Mr Williams was dark with a brown-tanned skin and almost black curly hair, this man was fair. A golden brown glazed his arms, and the hair on his head curled in tight yellow curls around a huge open face, with two piercing bright laser-beam eyes.

'Caught you a bit short did we?' the blond giant asked with a grin. 'Well, don't just stand there. Come back to the rig and explain yourself. We're all itching to know what you're about.'

His voice was friendly, but there was an underlying authority that warned Corey that he also meant what he said. Quietly he followed the giant back to the semis, where a group of drivers had gathered, waiting. Corey realized now where he had made his mistake; this man's rig had been a part of the huge convoy he had seen coming in to Port Wakefield from the west.

They were all fairly big men, and although none of them was anything like the size of the blond giant, they nevertheless towered over Corey, making him feel extremely small and helpless.

'Now then, lad, what's your name and what

are you up to? Straight, now . . .' the blond man demanded.

Corey's mind had been working rapidly for a few plausible reasons, but he had rejected each one of them as they had sprung to mind. Now he had to say something, and all that he had left was the truth.

'Corey Green', he mumbled. 'I've run away.'

For a moment no one spoke, then one of the men took Corey by the shoulder.

'That's a dumb thing to do, kid. It don't prove nothing, 'cept p'raps that you're weak.'

Corey flushed and stiffened with the insult, and the man's grip on his shoulder tightened but did not hurt.

'Well Dan, what do we do with him?' asked another. 'We can't leave him here, and we haven't time to go through all the rigmarole at the police station back there. The warehouse in Melbourne would be shut, and then we couldn't unload till Monday.'

Melbourne! Corey froze as he realized just how far away from home he was. His face paled. Dan ran a massive hand through his curly hair and narrowed his eyes while he thought. The other men stood waiting patiently. One lit a smoke.

'I'll take him with me', Dan finally said. 'Joe, you and the rest of the boys can go on to the warehouse as soon as we hit Melbourne and unload. I'll take this tacker along to the police station, and then come along afterwards. That'll give you time to unload and me time to hand him over and get back to the warehouse. What do you reckon?'

A rumble of agreement met this suggestion, and the men split up and wandered off toward their rigs. Dan turned to Corey.

'You're a right one, aren't you? How long have you been up there?' he asked, jerking his head toward the cars on the back of his rig.

Corey was trying desperately to put his thoughts into some sort of order. Dan intended to take him to a police station, probably in Melbourne. What would the police do? Again thoughts of having a criminal record made his eyes open wide.

'What? ... O, since last night, at Port Wakefield', he answered. Dan started in surprise, and then burst into a loud guffaw of merriment as he looked down at the boy. 'No wonder you were caught short, then', he laughed.

Corey said nothing, but to hide his embarrassment turned to pat Luke, the huge black dog, which was standing patiently behind him.

'You must have a way with animals, lad', Dan said. 'If anyone else had tried what you just did, Luke would have ripped their hand off at the elbow. I don't know what's got into him. Perhaps he's getting soft as he gets older, instead of tough.'

Corey still said nothing, so Dan turned with a

shake of his head and made for the semi, asking at the same time if Corey was hungry.

'Bit', Corey admitted.

The giant threw back his head and laughed. 'That'd mean you're starving, if my boys are anything to go by', he said, and pulled out an enormous box from somewhere in the truck.

'Here, have a feed on these, Corey lad, and don't stint yourself. There's plenty more where they came from.'

Corey took the box and lifted the lid. Inside were rows and rows of neat, but most definitely home-made, sausage rolls, and lying on its side next to them was a plastic sauce bottle with a pointed dispenser. Both nausea and hunger rose and fought for control in Corey's stomach as he reached in and took one, but after the first two bites, hunger won, and, forgetting everything but the food before him, Corey ate ravenously until he could eat no more.

Dan watched him curiously as he poured coffee from a thermos into two cups and handed one to the boy. Corey, his most urgent needs now dealt with, was sitting against the wheel of the rig with a worried crease on his brow.

'You've got yourself caught; now what are you going to do?' a voice in his head asked.

'Try to sneak away', Corey answered in his mind.

'Not going to be easy, especially if he drives you straight to a police station', the voice went on.

Sighing, Corey silenced the voice, for he had no answer for it. But he couldn't suppress a shudder or the tightening of all his insides as he thought of the trouble he was in for. Somehow, he decided, he just had to get away.

'Time to move', Dan said, and lightly sprang to his feet in a way that Corey would not have believed possible. The big man gathered up the cups and lunch box, and then gave a wave in the direction of the other men. Immediately they were all up and making for their rigs.

Inside the cab of the semi, Corey could not help but appreciate the rig. It was enormous and so high up that Dan had had to lift him to reach the cab. Even Luke had to crouch down and gather himself for the leap. The dashboard looked like something from the inside of an aeroplane instead of a truck, and dials and knobs, buttons and levers seemed to occupy every last centimetre within the considerable reach of the driver.

Corey could drive the farm ute at home and was familiar with the variety of ways that different vehicles were driven, but this . . . this was something else again. Under the dash was a rather complicated-looking two-way radio, and the little red light next to the microphone showed that it was running. The seat was a bench-type and, in keeping with the rest of the rig, enormous. Dan, behind the wheel, looked quite at home as he started the motor, and even Luke seemed content as he sat in the middle looking out of the front window with all the interest in the world. It was only Corey who felt small and out of place.

Dan didn't ask any questions, and Corey was grateful. He didn't want to explain all that had brought him here. What he did want was an idea or two on how he could get away, but no ideas came.

After half an hour's travelling, Luke grew bored with looking out the window and flopped down on to the seat with a grunt, dropping his head on to his massive forepaws and promptly going to sleep. Corey reached out a hand and stroked the short smooth hair on the dog's muscular neck, but Luke's only acknowledgment was a half-hearted lift of one eyebrow; his eyes didn't even open.

'How old is he?' Corey ventured, a trifle timidly.

'O he's not too old at all', Dan smiled. 'Just on two, I think. I breed Dobermans for a hobby and train them, or at least try to. I've never had one stand me up on a command yet, until today. You must be magic.'

Corey said nothing.

'Still, you can expect some slip-ups now and then, I guess. I'll just have to work on him some more before I sell him', Dan continued.

'Sell him!' Corey was surprised.

'Well of course, lad', the giant laughed. 'I can't keep all the dogs I breed; I'd have hundreds of them. I train them up for two or three years and then sell them, but I'm pretty particular about who they go to. I've got such a soft spot for them that I couldn't stand the thought of them being ill-treated. Luke's the last of this litter, but I'll have to keep him for a while yet, it seems.'

Corey couldn't help but like Dan. There was something so reassuring about him, so honest and open. The semi sped on. Kilometre after kilometre of farm country flashed past, and all the while Dan made easy conversation. Never once did he press Corey for any explanations or even ask where he came from, and the boy was feeling both very grateful and rather guilty that he didn't have to explain.

It was late afternoon when they finally reached the outskirts of Melbourne, and here the convoy split up. Joe called through on the two-way and told Dan he'd keep the warehouse open till he got there, and Dan said that he didn't expect to be too long, but if he was delayed he'd leave his load till Monday and not bother. As Dan hung up the microphone in its place, he turned to Corey with a half rueful look on his face.

'Sorry, mate, but I just can't leave you to go your own way', he said. 'Wouldn't be right, and I couldn't live with myself if I did, for wondering what had become of you.'

Corey hadn't quite thought of things that way, but it didn't change anything. He remained silent, and wondered rather desperately what he was to do. Melbourne traffic was like nothing

Corey had ever seen before. In frantic rushes, cars, vans, motorbikes, and even buses dashed and darted into impossible places around the stolid progress of the semi. It amazed the boy that something as huge as the rig could fit in a middle lane between two lines of traffic, and even more amazing was that nothing was ever collected when they turned a corner. And Dan, calm as ever, looked no different from when he'd been driving on the clear open road; the city traffic, it seemed, had no more effect on him that a flock of sparrows.

Gradually they left the worst traffic behind, and entered the suburbs. The roads, although still main artery roads, were now less congested and well monitored with traffic lights.

Corey wondered where they were going. Surely a police station would be nearer the centre of the city.

Finally they topped a rise, and began the long run down the other side toward what appeared to be another busy centre. The road ran down to an intersection where another major road crossed it, and Corey could see traffic lights blinking their tiny instructions to the cars.

Luke was sitting up again, intensely alert, his stubby tail wagging now and then as if he recognised home territory. Dan turned and playfully twisted the dog's ear; then he seemed suddenly to go rigid. Corey watched as the big man tried to brake again, but it was obvious that there was nothing to be felt. The rig's progress was not even checked, and the boy's mouth went dry as what this could mean sank in.

Dan didn't panic. The traffic lights in the distance turned red, and he was rapidly pushing buttons. Hazard lights suddenly began flashing, and the horn blared continually under the big golden-brown hand. Although the rig was moving at a good speed, Dan changed gears several times, making the engine almost scream in an effort to slow it. Still red, the traffic lights rushed closer with astonishing speed, and several cars in front of the semi shimmied out of the way like startled fish, but the traffic on the cross-roads was still unaware of the on-coming danger.

'Get on the fioor, boy, and stay there', Dan ordered, and Corey obeyed immediately. He was trembling, and his fingers dug so hard into the palms of his hands that his wrists ached with the strain.

Unable to see what was going on, Corey waited, wide-eyed and terrified. He could hear other horns blowing now, as if in defiance of the runaway rig.

Dan had changed down again, and the engine still screamed its protest. There was a swerve, another almost drunken lurch, and Dan muttered something as he threw himself sideways away from the wheel, and then they hit.

Whatever it was, it must have been solid, for the semi bucked hard, and the driver's side of the cab moved horrifyingly inwards as if some monster had pushed it in with its thumb. Glass splintered and then exploded everywhere, and the sound of the tortured engine suddenly cut dead. But they hadn't stopped moving. Momentum spun the back of the rig sideways, tipping it over, and with a screech of metal against concrete, the cab lurched crazily to one side. A great black weight pinned Corey down against the gears, and huge clawed feet scratched and bruised his arms and face as Luke scrabbled frantically for a foothold somewhere, and then, finally, everything was still.

Hardly daring to breathe, Corey looked up. The cab was not quite on its side, and Dan lay crumpled and twisted along the seat, his legs pinned at an almost impossible angle under the steering wheel, which had moved inwards, along with a lot more of the front of the truck.

Only the gear-box and console had saved Corey and Luke from being crushed as the front of the rig had been pushed in. Climbing upwards toward the door, Corey leant over and wound down the window. Luke leapt and was gone. Voices, cars, the hissing of hydraulics, and a babble of other noises crowded in from outside, along with a smell of diesel, exhaust fumes, and rain. Corey tried to think, but couldn't. Dan lay so still there on the seat, pinned and bleeding; perhaps he was even dead.

Instinctively Corey grabbed for his pack and

pulled it toward him, but it was stuck, a corner of it trapped under the dash somewhere, and he was denied even the comfort of hugging that while he thought. 'You've got to get away', the voice in his head said, 'get out of here and get away. The police will come. They'll want to know who you are, what Dan's name is, where he lives, *and you don't know*!'

Numbly Corey acknowledged the voice in his mind. Yes, he must get away. Leaving his pack he climbed out from under the dash and along the seat to the door, but he couldn't open it. The angle of the semi's cab made it impossible. He looked through the broken front window. People were climbing around the semi now, and someone called out: 'You hurt in there? Can you answer me?'

Corey didn't answer. Instead, he worked his way back toward Dan. He was very still but he was breathing, and Corey felt a wave of relief when he saw this. Outside, a siren was wailing in the distance, and the boy hoped desperately that it was an ambulance. Meanwhile he had to get away.

The cab was lying at an angle, not on its side but not on all its wheels either. Working his way back to the passenger door, Corey did as Luke had done, and climbed through the window.

As he emerged, the full impact of what had happened was suddenly made crystal clear to Corey. Dan, no doubt in a final attempt to avoid hurting anyone, had deliberately run into a

light pole. Although a great deal of the momentum had been checked by the time they collided, the impact had ripped the pole out of the ground, and now it was leaning backwards over the rig. Behind them the trailer had jack-knifed, but it had rolled too, and it was this which had caused the cab to tilt drunkenly on only two sets of wheels. A sudden, dreadful thought leapt into Corey's mind as he stared dazedly around at the chaos below him. If the impact had been straight, the trailer would not have jack-knifed; had Dan *deliberately* hit the light pole with the driver side of the rig? It certainly looked that way, and now he lay trapped, probably seriously injured, and Corey could do nothing.

'Strike me, lad, but you're lucky', a voice called softly. Corey spun around to see a man climbing toward him. 'Here, let me give you a hand down.'

Corey allowed the man to help him back to solid ground. People milled everywhere from cars and from the footpath, and nearby a crowd had appeared as if by magic. Two police cars were pulling up, sirens wailing, and one of the men quickly set about directing the clearance of traffic from further up the road, while another came toward the rig.

'Get out of here!' the voice in Corey's head screamed, and suddenly Corey obeyed. Twisting slightly out of the man's supportive grasp, he turned and ran.

'Hey . . .!' the confused man yelled, but he was too slow. Ducking and dodging, Corey was through the crowd before anyone realized what was happening, and by the time anyone did know, he was well on his way up the road. Several people set off after him, but Corey was an excellent runner and he'd had a good start; although he had no idea where he was going he continued to run, turning down different streets and roadways, until at last he was sure that no one was following him. Finally, gasping for breath and trembling violently, he stopped.

He was in a suburban area with houses lining a quiet roadway. It was dark now, and streetlights shone yellow at various intervals down the road. Corey walked miserably along until he came to a bus-shelter, and there he sat down. Then, miraculously, there was Luke, loping easily along the roadway some short distance behind.

As if sensing the misery and hopelessness which churned deep down inside Corey, the great black dog stood and looked at him for a moment. Then it lifted its front paws up on to the lad's knees, and leaning forward with something of an odd whine sounding in its throat, it offered the only comfort it had, a lick.

Full of misery and loneliness and fear, Corey put his arms around the dog and cried until there were no more tears left to cry.

CHAPTER 6

When he had finished crying, Corey just sat there, staring into space. He felt empty now, very empty and tired.

Luke still sat patiently at his feet, waiting. He looked as if he understood everything, and didn't mind the waiting at all. Corey gave the dog an absent pat and stood up. He had no idea where he was going, but he didn't want to stay in the bus-shelter any longer; he'd walk for a while and warm up.

It was indeed very cold, but it wasn't the sharp clear coldness of frost; it was a sort of damp cold that felt as if it had started from the inside, in the marrow of his bones, and worked outwards through his muscles and flesh. He was so cold inside that his body felt tight, too tight even to shiver.

Luke showed no feelings of cold whatsoever and walked quite contentedly beside Corey, his expressive ears twitching as he listened to the night sounds in the surrounding garden shrubs. Corey was glad the dog had found him, that he'd stayed and not run off again. They walked and walked, aimlessly. Corey had no idea where he would end up spending the rest of the night, and to put off thinking about it he just kept walking.

Gradually though, the exercise began to

loosen the tightness, and some warmth began stealing through the coldest parts of his body. He'd left the suburban area and turned on to a main artery road, but where it led to Corey had no idea, and nor did he care much.

It was a busy road, well lit with regular orange lights overhead. In the distance, the road looked rather like a bejewelled caterpillar, winding its exotic way toward a hazy glow, where hosts of other lights met in a warm, smudged blur. Other roads crossed or joined the one Corey followed, and traffic was continuously coming and going from it. Sometimes people would pass. An old woman with a large bag, obviously heavy, waddled along from a bus-stop, teenagers in pairs or small groups stood on corners, and sometimes even a boy or a girl would race along on a bike or skateboard toward a deli or a friend's place.

Corey saw all this, but he still felt somehow apart from it. The numbness which had set his body rigid was gone from everywhere except his head. He was hungry again, but there was nothing he could do about it. His money was still in his savings tin in his pack, and he'd left that in the rig. The thought of the rig immediately made him think of Dan. There was no way he would ever find out how he was. He knew nothing of Melbourne, and had no idea which hospital Dan would be sent to and no means of reaching it even if he did. He sighed, and kept walking.

The further he went the more traffic joined

the road, and Corey realized dully that he must be heading toward the city centre. More and more buildings were lit up, even though they were closed for business, traffic lights were more and more frequent, and the traffic was louder and more impatient. The road lost its importance as an artery road and became an inner-city thoroughfare, with other equally busy roads crossing it. Buildings were now ablaze with neon advertisements, and theatres, skating rinks, and ten-pin bowling alleys vied with each other for customers. Narrow doors, surrounded by brilliant lights, led into narrow passageways with steep staircases, richly carpeted, leading up to dimly lit, aromatic coffee rooms and clubs. Some delis were still open, and occasionally the smell of chips or onions would drift across Corey's path, making his mouth water. Music roared rhythmically from well-lit caves full of computer games, space invaders, and slot machines, and here teenagers wandered in and out in pairs or groups, laughing and chatting, smoking and jostling. Eight or ten bikies were sitting on motor cycles, laughing and cursing alternately, but no one paid any attention to Corey.

On he walked. A hot-dog stand made him hurry past, and then a Chinese restaurant, though he hated rice, made him double his pace. People were everywhere — noise, traffic, music, people. Melbourne, he decided, was the busiest place he'd ever seen.

Ahead were more caves with computer games, and outside every one of them was a crowd of young people. Across the road, two policemen walked casually, glancing now and then over the road toward the teenagers. A pang of fear shot through Corey, leaving a quick tingling wave of cold sweat behind it, but no one called out to him. Walking quickly, he put as much distance between himself and the policemen as he possibly could.

It seemed to be a very long road, but at last it appeared to peter out into a quieter section of the city, and for a while Corey stopped walking and wondered what to do with himself. Obviously he couldn't walk up and down all night, but what was the point of going on? It probably only led back to the suburbs.

'You need somewhere to sleep', the voice in Corey's head said, and somehow it sounded just like his mother's voice. Corey had no answer for it, but he set off again, anyway. He was coming to an older part of Melbourne. Many of the buildings here were made of corrugated iron instead of brick or cement, and the road was narrower. Lamp-posts stood at intervals, throwing a white circle of light around themselves, but after the warm orange lights of the highway and the neon of the city, these suddenly looked cold and forlorn.

Luke still trudged patiently along beside him, and Corey's hand dropped on to the dog's huge shoulders, as if seeking reassurance. The further they walked, the more run-down the area seemed to be. It was, without a doubt, a very old section of the city, and with the late hour and the streetlights fewer and further between, Corey couldn't help a feeling of apprehension crawling around the nape of his neck. It was a feeling which grew and grew with each passing minute, and miserable though he was, Corey's imagination was again beginning to stir. Melbourne was a pretty big city, and being near the sea there must have been boats calling in all the time. Perhaps the Russians had a ship just off the coast somewhere, a submarine, and they were going to sneak ashore and take hostages for ransom or something . . . This was the ideal sort of place to nab someone! Dark and dismal, it probably happened so much around here that the locals never bothered much when someone went missing. As long as it wasn't them. Dad had always said that most folk in the cities hardly knew their neighbours; why should they worry to check out the odd scream for help from someone they didn't know?

A small figure turned on to the road a short way ahead of Corey, and he quickly changed his idea from Russians to Chinese. The figure looked apprehensive, even from behind, and in the dark Corey couldn't tell whether it was a man or a woman. With quick short steps the little figure hurried forward, glancing back toward Corey from time to time, as if in fear that the boy was going to attack at any moment.

Corey, unknowingly, increased his speed a little. Ahead, the road came to a T-junction, and on one corner a solitary lamppost shed its mean circle of light on to the pavement. A stick-like figure leant against the lamppost with a lazy carefree attitude, obviously a man or a youth. He was smoking, the red of the lighted cigarette glowing hotly for a moment as he put it to his mouth. Hesitantly, the little Chinese in front of Corey glanced back and then forward again, the quick little steps faltering a little before surging on again.

The tall figure against the lamppost straightened. Corey slowed his pace as the little person ahead neared the light. Luke's hackles were bristling slightly, and a very low rumble echoed softly inside the dog's throat. Corey dropped his hand on to Luke's shoulder. Surely he wouldn't bound off and leave him now, he thought. Ahead, the tall figure had crossed the road, and the smaller one now seemed incredibly small indeed, as it cringed away from the taller one. Something didn't look right to Corey, and suddenly he knew why. The tall silhouette had grabbed the smaller figure, swung it around hard, and pushed it up against a fence. A short cry was quickly muffled, and the dark figure bent low, saying something to the other in deep gruff undertones. Apparently he was unaware that anyone else was around.

Corey watched, horrified. What could he do?

What should he do? He was only a boy, after all, and certainly no match for the huge shadow which was now threatening the smaller one.

'Better turn around and get out of here fast, before he spots you too', the voice in Corey's head advised. 'No good going on. That big Russian fellow will be finished with the Chinaman and ready for you by the time you get there.'

But somehow Corey didn't want to do that. Ignoring the voice, he kept walking toward the grim lamppost. An idea had crossed his mind. He didn't know, however, if Luke would work for him or not; if he did, then he might pull this off, but if Luke let him down as he had Dan . . . what then?

Crouching down beside the dog, Corey pointed to where the two argued in the shadows a little way away.

'The big one Luke, hold him', he whispered, and like a shot from a catapult the dog was gone.

For a moment Corey wondered if Luke would know what to do. Would he attack the right one? Had he, Corey, given the command properly? After all, he'd only heard Dan command the dog twice, and Dan himself had said that Luke was still unreliable . . .

Luke sprang, and suddenly a loud masculine scream split the air, followed by a stream of curses and horrible threats. Corey ran, but even as he arrived he could see that Luke had not let him down. In outright fear, the tall youth now lay

still, with Luke standing over him, his mouth loosely holding the fellow's arm, waiting for half an excuse to tighten the grip.

For the first time in what seemed an age, a grin spread over Corey's face. Dan would be proud of Luke tonight if he could see him. 'Come, Luke', Corey said, and the dog gracefully released the victim and came to stand obediently at Corey's side. Without a word, the youth clambered to his feet and was off, running as if the devil was after him. Corey turned to the silent figure beside him. In the darkness he still couldn't decide whether it was a man or a woman.

'You OK?' he asked.

'Yes, I am now, thank you', came the reply, and Corey knew instantly why this small person had been so apprehensive. It was a girl.

CHAPTER 7

'You're a girl!' Corey exclaimed, unable to help himself.

'So?' came the quick reply.

'Uh . . . I guess I'm just surprised. I thought you were a . . . a Chinaman', he explained lamely.

'A Chinaman? From China?' the girl asked.

'I was just daydreaming, I s'pose. Where are you going? Home?'

'Why?'

'Just wondering. I'll go with you, if you like.'

'Your dog's terrific. Is he yours? I guess he must be; dogs don't obey just anyone, do they? They have to have a master', the girl sighed.

'He's . . . not mine. He belongs to a friend . . . who's sick. I'm looking after him for a while', Corey said carefully.

Together the two began to walk along the roadway. It was still bitterly cold, but somehow Corey didn't notice it as much. Just having someone to talk to seemed to make all the difference.

'What did that guy want, anyway?' he asked.

'Money, but I don't have any. He didn't believe me. What's your name?'

'Corey Green. What's yours?'

'Tabatha Daniels', she answered grandly.

'Awful, isn't it? I usually get called Tabby for short. Anyhow, what're you doing around here this late at night? You don't live around here, do you?'

'I was just walking', Corey answered vaguely. 'Anyhow, what're you doing out this late?'

There was a moment's silence, and then the girl seemed to straighten herself, drew in a deep breath, and come to a decision. 'I've run away', she said, and to Corey's embarrassment she suddenly burst into tears.

Corey stood uncomfortably still on the pavement, trying desperately to control the feelings of shock, embarrassment, and indecision which surged around inside him. He knew better than anyone how this girl must be feeling, knew that she needed reassurance and comfort, but he was at a total loss as to how to go about giving it. When his sister, Linda, cried at home, he just left her to it, and usually when he cried he wanted to be alone anyway, but this girl wasn't his sister; he didn't know her at all, and somehow he couldn't bring himself even to try offering her his hand.

'C'mon, let's walk. You'll feel better in a minute', he said, but instead of sounding helpful and comforting, the words came out almost angrily. Tabby, however, did as he said, and after a while she had herself under control again.

'Sorry', she muttered.

''S OK', Corey answered.

'What are you going to do?' she asked quietly.

'Do? Nothing. Why?' Corey was surprised.

'Well . . . I mean, you must . . .' Clearly Tabby was confused. She had expected that Corey would try to find out where she lived and then take her home, but he had just kept walking on as if she had done no more than announce that the night was cold.

'Where do you live?' she asked, a little timidly, for although this lad wouldn't have been much more than a year or so older than herself, she suddenly felt very shy.

Corey looked at her with a wry grin, sighed, and said: 'South Australia. I've run away, too.'

Tabby gasped in surprise, and her eyes grew round and saucer-like as she looked back at him in the dimness.

'South Australia! That's miles away. Hundreds of miles!' she exclaimed. 'How did you get here?'

Suddenly Corey didn't feel like talking. To recount everything now, when he was so scared and everything still so raw inside, would only end up with him making a big fool of himself by crying again. And in front of someone he didn't know, and a girl too, that was as low as a fellow could go.

'It'd take too long for me to tell you tonight, and anyhow I've . . . we've got to find somewhere to sleep. You know of any cubbies round here?' he asked, not very hopefully.

'No, not really, but there's a salvage yard not far from here with a fence round it full of holes.

We might find something there', Tabby replied.

'OK. Let's try it.'

Together they set off along the dim forlorn streets, winding through narrow roadways past huge warehouses and factories. There were no houses at all now, and the two walked closely together, Corey with his hand on Luke's shoulder, feeling terribly small and insignificant against the huge black shadows which shrouded the buildings.

A fine drizzle of rain had started. Softly, like a heavy mist, it soaked everything within minutes, and Corey was continuously having to wipe the drips from his chin and nose, and squirm helplessly when it ran down his now-saturated hair, on to his neck, and on down his back. Tabby's plight was no different, but presently she turned along a narrow street and pointed ahead.

'It's down here', she said.

Sure enough, on their left they came to a break in the buildings. A tall wire fence ran from the end of the last building for a hundred metres or so to the corner of the block, and then turned and ran out of sight in the darkness the other way. Every metre or so a hole appeared in the fencing. Looking just as if someone had rolled a huge bowling ball through it, it seemed to bulge inwards and then burst apart. Little tracks in the dirt through these openings told of the regular traffic through each entrance. There was a cold white lamppost on the street at the corner of the block, but the light did little to illuminate any of what was inside the fence. Luke's hackles were prickling again, and he sniffed the air suspiciously.

'It's pretty dark', Tabby said in a small voice.

Tabby's fear made Corey more determined to hide his own. 'Yeah, c'mon', he said, and got down into a squatting position and waddled through one of the holes in the fence. Luke's liquid form flowed through and melted into the blackness like shadow into shade. Tabby crawled through on hands and knees, and hurried off after as much of Corey as she could see.

'There are some old cars and things in the far corner, I think', she whispered.

'Good idea', said Corey, and turned in the direction she had indicated. The going was not easy, and the further away from the light they went the worse it got. Huge piles of junk were everywhere, and they kept stumbling and tripping over lumps of metal, bricks, dirt, logs, stoves, and untold other things in the dark. Corey skun his shins, and Tabby grazed her hands and knees, and it was a full 15 minutes before they even came across a car.

Corey tried to peer through one of the windows. It was an old station wagon of some sort. Most of the bonnet and front section were missing, and even in the dark it had an air of wreckage about it, but to Corey it was as good as a feather bed.

'O Lord, let it be open', Corey silently prayed, and he reached out and tried the door.

It gave, and came open with a protest of grinding metal, which, to the two runaways, sounded loud enough to wake half of Melbourne. However, no one called out, and Tabby, Corey, and even Luke, all piled in.

It was very late, and Luke knew exactly what *he* wanted. Obviously he had travelled in station wagons before. In two bounds he was in the back section where he turned a circle and a half, sat down and scratched vigorously behind one ear, rocking the car violently in the process; then he flopped down unceremoniously, put his head on his paws, and promptly went to sleep.

Tabby and Corey could do nothing about their wet clothes, but it didn't really matter. It was dry in the car, and out of the rain it *felt* warmer. Tabby climbed on to the back seat and lay down with a sigh, and Corey did the same on the front seat. He was so tired. Too tired and miserable even to answer properly when Tabby called out goodnight to him. He just mumbled, and in spite of the wet and cold and discomfort he was asleep within moments.

CHAPTER 8

When Corey awoke, he was alone. Tabby and Luke were gone, and all around the station wagon, peering in at every window, were the sneering faces of a gang of grubby young lads. Without showing much of the fear which had suddenly tingled down his spine and landed hard in his gut, Corey looked back.

There were five of them, and they grinned widely at him while one opened the door and told him to get out. Carefully he did so, looking around and sizing up the situation at the same time.

'Who said you could use our cubby?' the tallest of the gang demanded. He would have been about 13, Corey judged, tall and lanky and obviously the leader.

Corey shrugged.

'This's our ground, kid. You've got no right to come in here without our say-so', the tall lad continued.

Corey still said nothing, but inside his head a voice was begging him to run. Now that it was daylight, Corey was able to see something of the salvage yard. Piles and piles of scrap metal were heaped up in rows, with narrow pathways winding between. Could Tabby be hiding somewhere? Where was Luke?

He remembered waking earlier. The sky, then, had been just tinged with red at the approaching dawn. Tabby had been trying quietly to get out of the station wagon without waking him.

'Where are you going?' he had asked.

'Outside. I've ... got to go', she had said.

Corey had lain down again and for a while stared up through the window at the gradually lightening sky. He must have drifted off to sleep again. All this seemed ages ago, but where were Tabby and Luke now?

A sudden blow to his shoulder put a stop to his silent questions, and he staggered back a pace or two, staring in surprised alarm at the black-haired lad who had hit him.

'Got no tongue, kid?' this second lad asked sarcastically. 'Where's your mum, then? Where you from?'

Corey continued backing, eyeing the advancing group of boys with wide eyes. He didn't mind a fight now and then; in fact, he picked them at school just for the fun of it sometimes, but five of them was a different story. A knot of fear began to tighten in his stomach. Where *was* Luke?

'What shall I do?' he asked himself silently, but the only answer he got was the voice inside his head, screaming at him to run, run.

So he did. He turned and ran, fast, and like a pack of dogs after a roo, the gang was after him, yelling with excitement.

Within seconds Corey was at the fence, but the first of the gang was too close. He would never be able to wriggle under before he was caught. Dodging quickly, he put the lad behind him and was again running fast through the maze of narrow pathways which wound between the mountains of scrap. His only hope was to reach a hole in the fence again, only this time further ahead of the gang so that he would have time to get through. But the plan was more easily thought of than carried out. Each time he got ahead, someone would take a short cut across his path, cutting him off, and it soon became obvious that they intended to corner him. Like the last king in a game of draughts, Corey was driven back, as each little pathway leading to the fence was systematically blocked. The gang closed in, and Corey, trapped with his back to the corrugated iron wall of a factory, gasped for breath, and watched fearfully and waited.

He didn't have to wait long. With a cry of victory, the gang attacked, punching, kicking, and even biting. Corey couldn't even try to fight back, as he sank under the flailing fists.

He must have fainted, because the next thing he remembered was waking up. At least the gang was gone. Carefully he moved an arm, opened his eyes, and blinked. He felt bruised all over.

'Hey, he's waking up!' someone said.

An arrow of fear shot into his stomach again; the gang hadn't gone, they were still here. No one touched him, however. Slowly he pulled himself into a sitting position, this simple action filling his head with blackness again. When it cleared, he looked around uncertainly, wondering what was going to happen next, and for a moment he saw nothing but the scrap iron of the salvage yard. Then he looked at the station wagon, and, in spite of everything, very nearly laughed.

On its roof sat all five members of the gang, watching him almost hopefully. Several of them nursed bloodied hands and arms, and they were all sitting remarkably still for boys. Luke was back.

Corey climbed on to his feet, something which proved harder to put into action than he'd ever thought possible, and made his way unsteadily toward the dog. With a crooked glance at the five boys on the roof of the wagon, he told them to stay where they were, then he hugged Luke as if he'd never let him go.

A wave of sickness washed through him, and he had to sit down again. He felt horribly thirsty and very very sore. One of the gang on top of the station wagon squirmed, and at once Luke's hackles were raised; his mouth drew back in a very ugly snarl, revealing long white fangs, and a deep growl rumbled warningly in his throat. The boy froze, and Corey did nothing to relieve the boy's discomfort, not because of any feelings of revenge, but because he really was feeling rather ill, and the trouble it would take to tell Luke to be quiet was more than he could manage at that moment. He hated being sick, hated even feeling sick, and the only way he could combat the nausea was to lie down again until he felt better. His stomach growled and rumbled, and his head was dizzy, but he did feel much better once he lay flat and closed his eyes. The gang would just have to wait.

When Tabby returned half an hour later, Luke was still guarding the gang on top of the station wagon, though not so obviously. The lads, however, were not about to try to escape, and Corey was apparently having another sleep, right in the middle of the salvage yard.

Realizing that something was wrong, she hurried awkwardly through the hole in the fence, juggling an armful of packages at the same time. 'Corey', she called as she ran, 'Corey, what's happened?'

He opened his eyes and looked up at Tabby uncomprehendingly at first; he had not seen her in daylight. Then he seemed to recognise her.

'Where have you been?' he asked absently.

'I went to fetch something to eat and drink. I told a fib when I said I had no money last night, but that was only because I wasn't sure of you at first. Anyway, I wanted to surprise you with breakfast. Who are they?' she finished a little breathlessly.

'I dunno', Corey answered. 'That's their cubby, anyhow, and they didn't like me sleeping there. Did Luke go with you?'

'No, not really. When I climbed out this morning he squeezed out before me and bounded off on his own somewhere. I thought he just wanted to run around, so I didn't try to catch him again. Why?'

Corey was secretly delighted at this news, but he kept it to himself. 'He wasn't here when I woke up, but the gang was. We had a fight, and I suppose Luke must have come back in the middle of it. When I woke up they were all up there, and Luke was keeping guard', he told her.

Corey was beginning to feel a bit better now, although the sick feeling hadn't quite left his stomach.

'What did you bring to eat?' he asked, suddenly feeling shy.

'Some buttered rolls, two oranges, and a bottle of Coke', she answered, and set about organizing her packages, which she had dropped when she found Corey.

'What are you going to do with *them*?' she asked, nodding in the direction of the station wagon.

Corey pulled himself into a sitting position, leant back against an old piece of iron, scratched his neck and his head, and sighed. There was lots he would *like* to do to them, but what was the use? He hadn't the energy. He scratched his head again, and then said: 'Come,

Luke.' The huge dog left his post with pleasure, and came to sit beside Corey.

'You lot can get lost', he told the gang, and then watched with grim satisfaction as they gingerly climbed down from their island of safety. Keeping wary eyes on the dog, the five stuck very close to each other, and, ever ready to run should it become suddenly necessary, they almost tiptoed away.

Tabby passed a bread roll to Corey, and then dug deep into another of her parcels. What a god-send, Corey thought, as he watched her pull out a piece of meat for Luke. That was one of his mother's sayings when someone came up with what was really needed just at the right time; suddenly he felt very homesick.

To cover his troubled thoughts he bit into the bread roll, and discovered, after the first mouthful, just how hungry he was. Together they sat and munched in silence until there was nothing left.

'That was good', Corey said, leaning back on his scrap iron again, and he did really feel very much better. Who would have thought that a simple bread roll and an orange could do so much? Now he sat watching Tabby as she finished her orange. He hadn't been able to see much of her in the dark the night before, and he had been surprised when he had seen her in daylight. She had short hair, red and curly, and it surrounded a pretty face which was sprinkled softly with freckles. Her eyes were green, and her smile quick. There was nothing at all to her size, but she had something which made you take notice. Somehow she shone, like sunshine.

'Well, what are you going to do now?' Tabby asked, as she packed all the orange peel and paper into one bag.

Corey shrugged. 'Dunno. How come you ran away?' he asked suddenly.

Tabby sighed and sat back against another piece of scrap, facing him.

'It's funny, really. I haven't really run away. Well, I have and I haven't. It's all so complicated. Mum and Dad . . . they don't always exactly get on.' She sighed and stared at a point somewhere distant, above Corey's head. For a while he wondered if that was all she was going to tell him. Then she continued.

'Dad's an alcoholic. He can't go a day without a drink. Once . . . he used to be such fun, but then he quit work and we had to go on the dole. We lost our house because Mum said we couldn't afford to keep up the payments, and then we moved down here. That's when Dad started going to the pub. It's right next door, you see, and he often comes home tiddly. Mum used to get cross, but it made no difference. She says it's boredom that makes him do it. That was two years ago, and now . . . well, he's just not the same any more. Not long ago, about three months I suppose, he came home really drunk and bashed Mum up. She says he doesn't know what he's doing when he's drunk, and I must forgive. He doesn't talk much to me any more, and I don't hang around when he's home anyway. Last night, though, was the worst I've seen him ever. He was so cross. Someone at the pub had had a fight with him and told him he was nothing but a drunken dole-bludger or something.

'At first he was only ranting and Mum kept quiet and started the dishes, but we guessed it was going to get worse. When it was bedtime Mum came up and gave me $20.00. "If there's another fight tonight, you get out, Tabby, and find a taxi. Go to your grandmother's. Can I trust you, now, not to let me down? Go there and I'll come as soon as I can, all right?" And that's just what I did, except that fellow cut in as I was making my way to a phone box to call a taxi, and then you and Luke came along.'

Corey was shocked. Poor Tabby, what a dreadful time she must have had. Thinking back, Corey couldn't remember his parents ever fighting. Oh, they were irritable with each other sometimes, but they didn't 'fight', not yelling and screaming and stuff like that. The thought of Dad ever hitting Mum horrified Corey as nothing else ever had.

'Why didn't you tell me last night? I could have walked to a phone box with you', he said.

'I guess I just didn't want to be on my own again in the dark. It . . . it was sort of safe, with you and Luke. What about you? Why have you run away?'

Now it was Corey's turn to stare at some invisible point overhead. Compared with Tabby's, Corey's reasons suddenly seemed very selfish and weak. A semi driver's remark echoed in his head. 'That's a dumb thing to do, kid. It don't prove nothing, 'cept p'raps that you're weak.'

A horrible feeling grabbed the pit of Corey's stomach and squeezed. He *had* been weak. Weak as water — and this girl here had more guts than he'd ever have if he didn't sort a few things out. What was he running from, anyway? A few hundred lines. Discipline. The fact that he'd got the cane. Discipline. His parents' anger and disappointment. Discipline. And they were angry because they cared, because it mattered to them how he would grow up. If he couldn't hack a few hours of school every day, how on earth was he going to cope with a regular job? He might turn out like Tabby's father ... or worse. And what had running away proved? Again an echo: 'Not the things I wanted it to prove.' In fact, running away had caused him more hardship and pain than if he'd stayed where he was and faced up to everything. Hadn't it been his own selfish pride that had prevented him ringing up Mum from Port Wakefield? And now, even after all this, the consequences were still there to be faced.

Very slowly, hesitatingly at first, he began to tell Tabby everything, and, listening to himself talking, he found himself squirming inwardly in some places. It sounded very different out loud from the way it had felt in his head. He left nothing out, though, and when he'd finished he just sat there, looking down at his feet, feeling very stupid and ashamed and *weak*.

Tabby said nothing, and Corey looked up after a while. He was surprised and further shocked to see her hastily wiping away a tear.

'Do you believe in God?' she asked suddenly.

'Huh? ... I guess so. I must, I suppose, because when things got really rotten, I'd sometimes ... well, sort of pray.'

'Mum says that we only see what we want to see. We lie to ourselves so much that it's often hard to find the real truth, and even when those who love us try to tell us, we don't always want to hear. But God can show us in such a way that we can't fail to see that something is true, and I think that's what has happened to you.'

Corey sat up and digested this. Could it be that the girl was right? He got up.

'Come on', he said.

'Where are we going?' Tabby asked.

'To your grandmother's', he answered, and set off immediately toward a hole in the fence.

CHAPTER 9

Tabby's grandmother, Mrs Purvey, was a very straight woman. She walked erect, her hair was pulled back firmly to a grey bun, and her steel-grey eyes looked right into you.

They had arrived at Mrs Purvey's at around 11, and while Tabby explained everything that had happened, the old lady had continued to study Corey and Luke so closely that Corey was soon feeling very uncomfortable. When she had heard Tabby's story, though, Mrs Purvey spoke directly to Corey.

'You are the boy who was travelling in the semi-trailer which crashed yesterday, aren't you?' she stated.

Corey looked up in shocked surprise. However did she know?

'H . . . how did you know?' he stammered.

Mrs Purvey nodded to a newspaper lying face downwards at the other end of the table. Corey got up and went to it, looked at Mrs Purvey, who nodded to him to carry on, and turned it over. Tabby came to stand beside him.

Half of the front page was filled with a picture of a smashed and buckled semi, surrounded by cars. Cars were all over the place, some crashed, some run into the back of others, and the car Corey had hidden in before Luke had 'caught' him was lying on its side on top of another. The headlines spelt out a message in huge capitals: 'HAVOC REIGNS AS SEMI CRASHES AT INTERSECTION'.

Corey sat down with a thump. He read on, not really wanting to, but knowing he had to. There was an account of the injuries, the number of vehicles directly involved, and theories about the cause of the crash. No one had died. There was a footnote, too.

> It is believed that a boy who has been reported missing from his home in SA since Thursday was also travelling in the vehicle. A knapsack with the name Corey Green on it was found in the cab, and one of the first people on the scene claims to have seen a boy and a black dog leave the semi and run off. It is important that this boy is found and brought to the nearest police station for questioning.

Corey went white and swallowed hard. He looked at Mrs Purvey, his blue eyes larger and rounder than ever. Now the police were really after him.

'Have you ... called the police?' he asked hesitantly.

'Not yet.' He frowned and stared hard at the corner of the table. A squeak in his head tried to say 'run', but he squashed it before it really began.

'But you can't be going to phone, Grandma!' Tabby exclaimed. 'After all he's been through, all he's done for me . . .'

'That's quite enough, young lady. You know as well as I do that people must face up to their responsibilities. Now, young man, I expect you'd like a wash . . .'

Mrs Purvey led the way to a small bathroom.

'After you've cleaned up, come back to the kitchen and have something to eat', she said, not unkindly. Corey, however, had no doubts at all that while he was cleaning up, Mrs Purvey would be quickly dialing for the police.

He stared at himself in the mirror. His blond hair, usually fine and shining was now dull, and stuck out in tufts from his head. His face was grubby and bruised, and dried blood still stuck to his upper lip and cheeks. His body ached horribly. He ran some water into the basin and, using the face washer, quickly washed his face. With the hair brush on the vanity bar he brushed the worst of the tufts from his hair, discovering more tender spots in the process, and then he let the water go from the basin.

'You'll have to go, Corey', Tabby whispered from the doorway. 'I'm really sorry, but she's phoning the police now. They'll be here at any time, and with Luke in tow you'll be easy to spot. If you don't get a good start now . . .'

Corey twisted his face into a grimace. 'I guess so', he answered.

'Where will you go?' Tabby asked.

'The paper named a hospital. I'm going to try to see how Dan is first, find out where . . . where to take Luke. Then I suppose I'll give myself up.'

'I'll miss you. It's been a real adventure in a way, hasn't it? Corey . . . would you write, just once, to let me know where you are . . .?'

'I guess so. Yes, yes, course I will.'

'Here, use this address.' Tabby pressed a sheet of folded writing paper into Corey's hand, hugged him briefly, and then fled out of the bathroom and down the passage to disappear into another room.

Corey, blushing hotly, made his way back to the kitchen. Mrs Purvey was putting down the phone. She turned toward him.

'I'd like to thank you for looking after Tabatha . . .' she began stiffly.

''S OK', Corey answered.

'Would you like something to eat?' she asked.

'No. I'll get going now', he said calmly.

'But I've just phoned for the police', she said, and then sighed. 'It really would be better in the long run, Corey, if you faced your troubles. They are over and done with much more quickly that way . . .'

'I am facing them. It's just not in the same order, that's all', Corey answered, and, followed closely by Luke, he opened the front door and set off without a backward glance.

The moment he was out of the front gate, however, he started to run. The police would come along this road at any time now, and if he were caught he would be well and truly finished. He ran and ran, keeping a sharp lookout in all directions, until, at last, he was reasonably sure that he was safe. Then, taking refuge in a bus-shelter, he sat down to catch his breath while he decided what to do. His body ached, his split lip throbbed, and he felt as if everything was closing in on him much too quickly. He was a wanted person now, a criminal, and it didn't feel one bit as it looked in some of the movies on TV.

Luke sat obediently beside him, and Corey absently stroked the dog's head. However would he have managed without Luke? It wasn't going to be easy giving him back. A lump rose in Corey's throat, and to take his mind off such thoughts he pulled out the folded paper Tabby had given him. There was an address, a small note, and ten dollars. 'Take this, Corey. It's the change from Mum's $20.00. You may need it. Don't forget to write, will you? Love, Tabby.'

Another lump came to Corey's throat, but an idea quickly followed it. If he could get to a main road and find a taxi, he might still reach Dan at the hospital before the police finally caught up with him.

The taxi put him down in front of a huge, multi-storeyed building. The double-doored entrance was rather formidable, and Corey nearly had second thoughts about going in. But then his resolve strengthened; taking a deep breath, he told Luke to sit, and went inside.

There were people everywhere, and huge

signs pointed to different sections of the hospital. He found one which said 'Enquiries', and followed it to a long counter full of information leaflets. There he waited. The air smelled of disinfectant and carbon paper, and it was very warm. Finally a nurse came and asked him if she could help.

'I want to know which room a man called Dan is in', he explained. 'He's a semi driver, and he was in a crash the other day.'

'Are you a relative?' the nurse asked, looking at him suspiciously.

'No.'

'Well, I'm not sure . . .'

'Look, I'll only be there a minute or two. I've got to see him. I have something that belongs to him. He may want it back now, may be worrying about it.'

'Well . . .' She referred to a large black book. 'He's in room 231 on the ground floor. It's easier to go around the side entrance off the road that comes from the car park. Go in that door and turn left. Then go down the corridor until you see a set of lifts. It's about the third or fourth room down on the left after those. If he's not in his room, he may be down in the TV room, which is right at the end of that corridor. OK?'

'Thanks', Corey said, and bounded off out of the door again. He was feeling greatly cheered as he and Luke headed off to the left around the hospital. If Dan was not confined to his room, then he was obviously not dying.

The directions the nurse had given were quite clear, and the boy had no trouble at all finding the side entrance. He pushed the door open and peered inside. No one was in sight, so he held the door open and softly called Luke in. Quickly the pair of them made their way down the corridor toward the set of lifts which could be seen about half way along. Still no one approached, but suddenly a lift arrived. Corey froze and grabbed Luke's collar. The doors swished apart and stayed there, but no one came out. Carefully Corey edged forward until he could see right inside. It was empty. Breathing a sigh of relief, he hurried past. He had to find Dan's room before someone else arrived.

Room 231, and another lift sighed into place. There was no time to knock or call, so, grabbing the door handle, Corey barged in with Luke just as the lift doors opened and two nurses walked out.

Behind the closed door of 231 Corey relaxed and breathed a deep sigh. He was, temporarily, safe, but Dan wasn't here. The bed was neatly made, and the locker beside it rigorously tidy. Opposite the door a huge window opened out on to the garden area through which Corey had just passed in order to reach the side door. Luke, however, was getting excited. On the floor was a huge pair of boots, and the scent had the dog half whimpering as it sniffed and resniffed around the room, its huge body wagging as much as its stub of a tail. There was no doubt at all that this was Dan's room.

Still, safe as it was here in 231, Dan could be in the middle of an epic movie down in the TV room, and if that was the case, Corey didn't have time to wait. Luke belonged to Dan, and Corey's responsibility, as he saw it, was to return the dog to its owner, and he felt he had to do that himself. It was little enough after all Dan had been through.

He couldn't ask anyone else to deliver the dog because he didn't know where Dan lived. No, this was the only way; he would not go to the police until the dog was safely in the hands of its rightful owner.

Corey opened the door, peered out again into the corridor, and found it empty. It was now or never. This time, though, they weren't so lucky. Just as Corey was about to open the door to the television lounge, a stout nurse came out of one of the rooms.

'Good grief, child, whatever do you think you're doing? Get that filthy animal out of here at once', she said.

'I've got to see someone first', Corey answered firmly.

The nurse's mouth pulled itself into a straight line, and the pale blue eyes became frosty. 'Well I'm afraid that's just too bad, young man. You can't go bringing dogs into the hospital. There are sick people here, and dogs carry germs. Besides, it's against the rules', she finished, looking extremely hostile by now.

'I want to see Dan first', Corey stated stubbornly.

'I've had enough of this. Now you do as you're told and get that creature out of here, or else I'm going to get cross', the nurse said irritably.

'What's going on here, nurse?' a voice said, and Corey's heart sank as he looked up to see a doctor approaching.

'This . . . this boy, refuses to take this dog out of the hospital', the nurse exclaimed, almost spluttering at the affront.

'Can't have dogs in here, son', the doctor said amiably. 'Better take it outside.'

'I have to see someone first. It will only take two minutes and then I'll go, but this is important.'

'I'm not interested in how important it is, that dog's got to go . . . Hey, I know who you are! You're the kid in the crash . . .' the doctor began, but Corey interrupted.

'Hold them, Luke', he commanded calmly. Then he turned, pushed the door to the TV lounge open, and walked in.

It was not a large room, but several chairs were placed in rows around a large TV screen which was bolted on to the wall. Several patients turned to look as Corey entered, but then turned back to the picture again as the door closed. It was easy to find Dan. He towered above everyone else, even when sitting. Corey made his way around the chairs toward him. He was sitting in a wheelchair, but Corey could not see if there was plaster on his legs or not.

'Dan?' he said quietly.

The giant looked around, surprised.

'Corey? Corey Green. But what are you doing *here*?' he asked.

'Shhhh', one of the patients hissed.

'Let's go back to my room; we can talk there. Will you push?'

Corey stepped behind the wheelchair and manoeuvered it out of the TV area, toward the door.

'Er, Dan, I'm afraid this is going to cause some trouble', Corey said.

'What is? Just wheel the thing through the door. It swings both ways.'

'No. I mean what's on the other side of the door', Corey answered, and with that he pushed the chair through.

Luke was indeed well practiced at 'holding' people, but at the sight of Dan the spell was very nearly broken. Whimpering painfully, the poor dog alternately squirmed with joy and snarled his captives back into place, until Corey could stand it no longer.

'Come, Luke', he said, and, thus released, the grateful animal flew up on to the wheelchair in sheer delight.

'Luke', Corey screamed, grabbing at the dog's collar. 'Luke, get *down*! You'll hurt him. O please, Luke', he called over and over. 'Down Luke', Dan said quietly, and immediately the dog obeyed. 'Calm down, Corey', he told the boy. 'My legs are OK. I just had concussion. I'm in this thing merely to please the nurses.'

Corey made a valiant attempt to pull himself together.

'Now perhaps you'll understand why dogs aren't allowed in hospitals, young man. If Mr Williams's legs had been damaged in that crash, that dog could have crippled him for life', the nurse began acidly.

'That's enough, nurse', Dan cut in sharply. 'We'll go out into the garden, and you needn't bother yourself any more about the dog. I'll take full responsibility for everything from now on. Come on, Corey, wheel me to the side door up there, and then we can talk.'

Mutely, Corey did as he was told, leaving a fuming nurse and a secretly rather amused doctor in their wake.

CHAPTER 10

'Phew, you've really been a busy fellow, haven't you?' Dan remarked some time later after Corey had again told his tale. 'But I reckon it's made a man of you.'

Corey looked down at his feet, feeling embarrassed. He couldn't really see how his actions had made a man of him at all.

'You don't believe me, do you? But it's true. It takes a lot of guts to admit you're wrong. What are your plans now?'

'I'll go to the police, I suppose, and sort things out there.'

'And then?'

Corey shrugged. 'I think . . . I want to go home.' There was suddenly a lump in his throat as he thought of home. In a week, maybe, everything would be back to normal. Well, nearly normal. Things would be different too, he decided, because inside he had changed. But would his parents *want* him back? They'd loved him and cared about him once, but had he thrown all that away when he'd left home? Perhaps they wouldn't want to trust him with their love any more. He could only try . . . and perhaps pray. Yes, he would pray. It had worked before. Now, suddenly, some of the things that he had been told in RI lessons made sense. Funny how he didn't seem to hear that voice in his head so much any more.

'Dan?'

'Yes.'

'Do you talk to yourself, in your head I mean?'

'Yes, I think everyone does. It's you telling yourself what you want, most of the time. Why do you ask?'

'Usually it gets me into strife, but just lately it's shut up, and I was sort of wondering how come.'

'Do you believe in God?' Dan asked.

'Yes.' Corey's answer was more definite this time.

'Well, it's like this', Dan said. 'We always think about ourselves and what *we* want, but God's Holy Spirit is trying to make us think about other things — about what God wants and what other people need. God sent Jesus to die for us, and he loves us and wants to change us, but he won't force us. You can choose the devil's way by carrying on about yourself all the time, and end up in the sort of mess you're in now, or even worse. Or, you can let God work in you and end up with peace and joy in your head and your heart. But it's not always easy. God disciplines us, and sometimes it hurts, but if it brings us back to him it's worth it.'

A silence fell between them then, and Corey knew that it was time to leave. Steeling himself, he asked: 'Would you like me to take Luke to your house? It wouldn't be any trouble. I can't leave him here really, not when he's not allowed in the hospital.'

'No, lad, my wife and boys will be along to visit in half an hour. I'll stay here with him till then, and they can take him home. You have enough on your plate for now. You still have to visit the police station yet', Dan replied.

Corey nodded. The lump in his throat seemed to have doubled in size, and he knew that if he said one more word he would burst into tears. Instead he turned away; roughly attempting a careless wave to Dan, he ignored Luke completely, and with a superhuman effort he walked away, as casually as he could, leaving behind him two of the most treasured friends of his life.

Luke whined and stood up, watching intently after the lad, but Dan had a firm hold on his collar, and the dog could do no more than utter a short yelp before sitting down again to watch the pathway along which Corey had disappeared.

Out of sight at last, Corey let go of the tears that he had been holding back. Ignoring the 'Keep off the grass' sign, he shot across to some oleander bushes where he would not be seen. He didn't cry for long, though. Somehow he soon found that he was praying. He told God everything, and asked him to make it all somehow turn out right. He was sick of running away and causing trouble, even unintentionally. He wanted Mum and Dad, and he was terribly afraid that they would never want to see him again.

Finally he calmed down. His tears had gone, but he still had things to do. There were still consequences to face, and the sooner he got on with the job the quicker things would be sorted out. He stood up, made his way out of the hospital grounds, and turned left on to a pathway that he hoped would lead to a policeman. Instead, it led to someone else. It led to Mr Williams. Corey looked up, and the dark mountain of a man looked down, recognition spreading like sunshine across his face.

'Wh ... what are you doing here?' Corey asked.

'My brother Dan is in hospital here. I came over to see if he's all right. What are you doing here?' Mr Williams asked.

Dan? Dan Williams? They were alike in some ways; was it possible?

'Your parents are here, Corey. When your pack was found in Dan's rig, I arranged for them to travel with me in case there was any news.'

'Mum and Dad?' Corey asked carefully. 'Are they ...? I was going to find a policeman, give myself up and then ... well, go home.'

'Good for you, but you won't need to see a policeman now. We can ring from the hotel and tell them you've been found.'

'But the newspaper ...?'

'I know, but that was because no one knew what had happened. Dan was still unconscious when that went into print. Now, of course, the whole story's cleared up, except for the fact that we couldn't find you. Anyway, let's get you back to your parents.'

Corey both hated and loved seeing his parents again. He hated seeing the strain he had caused, which had pinched their cheeks and creased their eyes, he hated the tears he couldn't hold back, he hated the hurt and worry and pain that he had caused them. But he loved them. And best of all, they still loved him, very much. It was terrible really, what they had been through, but even though he was so upset about what he had done, underneath, in a very deep place inside him, he was singing. Was this what Dan had meant when he had spoken of peace and joy? Corey was a changed person now, and in the future that change was going to show, and inside he realized that it was the kind of change that would make his parents happy.

It was Thursday. Lessons had been particularly trying that morning, especially music with Miss Bavistock, but somehow Corey had managed to stay out of trouble. The day dragged on to RI, which was now a lesson Corey didn't mind, and then, at last, school was out. The first footy practices of the season were starting today, but strangely, Corey felt no stir of excitement as he climbed aboard the bus which would take him home. Somehow he felt flat. It wasn't that he was unhappy — just the opposite — but there was a little ache inside which gave a twinge whenever he saw a black dog. He tried to put the thought of Luke aside; Dan had probably sold him by now.

The bus pulled up at the Greens' stop, and Corey and his brothers and his sister all piled out and started off up the driveway home. They were almost there when suddenly Linda yelled out.

'Look out, that dog! It's going to attack someone . . .' she almost screamed.

Corey looked up, just as Luke leapt. The huge creature was beside itself with excitement, whining and wagging its huge body from side to side as it licked Corey almost from head to foot.

'Down, Luke, down!' Corey yelled, and very reluctantly the animal sat, its whole body still wagging with excitement. Corey struggled to a sitting position, as his brothers and his sister looked on in wonderment. Tears were streaming down Corey's cheeks, as half sobbing and half laughing he hugged the dog.

'Well, I'll be!' exclaimed Linda. 'Where on earth did that come from?'

'Someone in a semi called in today, and dropped it off for Corey, on condition that it was OK with his parents. It's for him to keep. There's a letter, too', Mum said, appearing on the verandah.

Quickly Corey tore open the envelope.

'Dear Corey', it read. 'Just a quick note to explain. Luke wouldn't settle. He was pining for you, just as I imagine you would be pining for him. I know you will take very good care of him, and he of you, so he's all yours, if you want him. Will call in on the way back from the West. Meanwhile, God bless you. Dan.'

'Yipeeeee!' Corey howled ten minutes later, as he and Luke set off down the drive for footy training, and there was no one in the whole wide world who could have been happier then than Corey Green.

The author, Mrs E.J. Davis, has lived at Poochera, a small town on Eyre Peninsula, South Australia, for about 18 years. She works at the nearby Karcultaby Area School as a Teachers Assistant. She loves the outdoors, and enjoys exploring the local region, often in the company of young people. Other hobbies are fishing and horse-riding.

If you have enjoyed this book,you will also want to read E.J. Davis's *Trouble with Linda*, a story about Corey's sister.